Jane *and the* Storm

Angela Reynolds, Ed.D

AuthorHouse™
1663 Liberty Drive
Bloomington, IN 47403
www.authorhouse.com
Phone: 1 (833) 262-8899

This book is printed on acid-free paper.

ISBN: 978-1-7283-7105-4 (sc)
978-1-7283-7104-7 (e)

Print information available on the last page.

Published by AuthorHouse 09/02/2020

authorHOUSE®

"Never let other people's
fears become your own.
Have your own experiences."

For my children
Jaron**, **Chad**, and **Madison
who fill the room with their
love, intelligence, and
energetic natures.

Jane looked out the window of her house. The sky was overcast and the clouds were beginning to turn gray. It would be two more hours before the storm made landfall in Jamaica.

Jamaica was one of the Caribbean Islands in the Western Hemisphere that seemed a target for storms.

Mrs. Peggy, Jane's mom came into the living room. "We need to go to the supermarket," she said. "There is no food in the house." "We are going to need some water, candles, and batteries too."

"Well, let's go before it starts raining," said Jane.

Mrs. Peggy and Jane began walking down the road to the supermarket. They saw people preparing for the storm. Some people did not seem to care about the storm.

As they continued walking, they saw one of their neighbors, Mr. Joe filling up a drum with water. His brother was nailing pieces of wood to cover the windows and doors.

"Jane!" Peter shouted. Peter attended the same elementary school as Jane. "How is it going with your preparations for the storm?" "We are going to get some groceries before the storm arrives," said Jane. "Ok, see you later," said Peter.

Mrs. Peggy and Jane finally arrived at the supermarket. They picked up some food items, candles, batteries, and bottled water. Mrs. Peggy paid for the groceries, candles, and batteries while Jane placed them in the shopping bags. Then they hurried home.

M&S CLOUGH SUPERMARKET
pples 50¢ per doz
CORN OIL
$20 per gall.

ENTRANCE

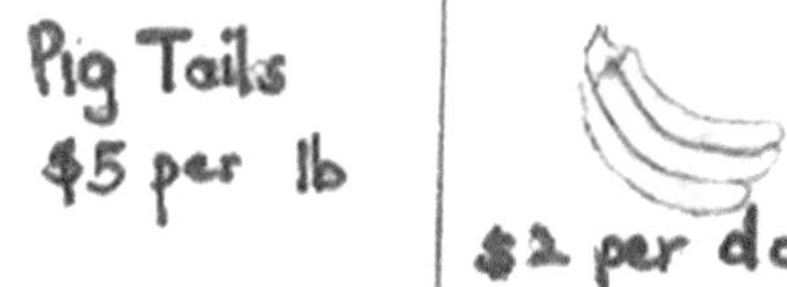
Pig Tails
$5 per lb
Bananas
$2 per doz.

Splitter! Splatter! Splash! The heavy rains came pouring down. The wind howled and the trees swayed.

"This is so exciting!" Jane shouted. It was her first time experiencing a storm. "Wait until I return to school on Monday! I'm going to write a great story!"

Suddenly! The roof started leaking. "Oh no! What are we going to do?" said Jane. "Go and get some containers to catch the water as it drips," said Mrs. Peggy. Meanwhile, Mrs. Peggy started moving the furniture away from the leaky spots.

It seemed as if the rain was inside the house and not outside. After reorganizing the furniture, and making sure everything was alright, Mrs. Peggy and Jane sat down.

"Mom, look out!" said Jane. The wind had blown a part of the roof from Mrs. Peggy's bedroom. Mrs. Peggy moved quickly. She pushed the furniture into the living room and closed the bedroom door. Then she placed the bookshelf behind the door.

It seemed as if they had now passed the worst. Suddenly, the lights went out. "Oh my!" said Jane. "Quick Jane! Go and get some candles," said Mrs. Peggy. Jane went to get the candles. Her mom lit them. The living room became filled with light.

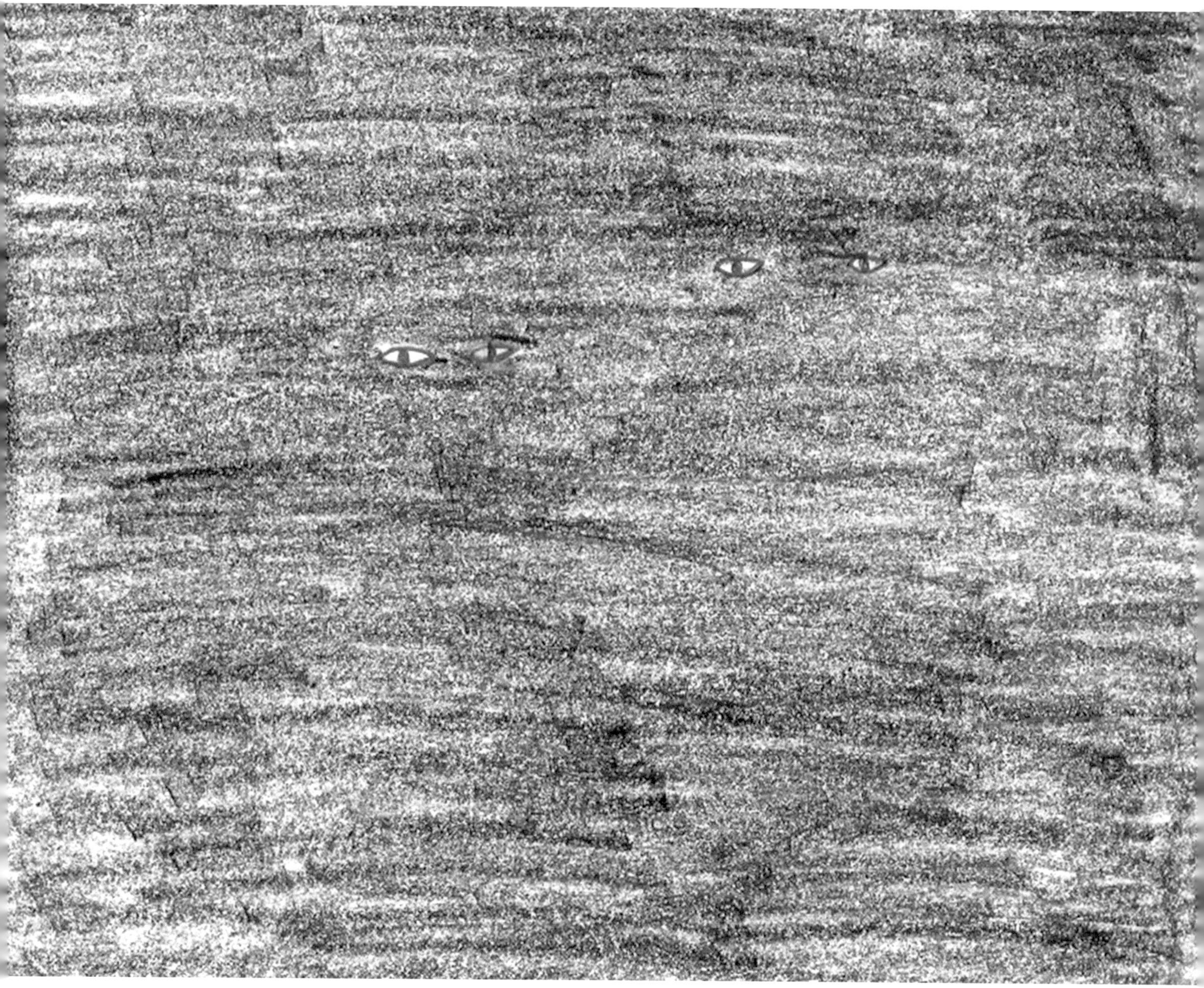

Finally, it seemed like they had everything under control.

"Well, I guess there is nothing more we can do," Jane said to her mom. "Let us go to our beds. Tomorrow will be a brand new day."

And a brand new day it was, indeed!

Teaser for Upcoming Series Book 2

"What is that?" said Jane. Lisa and Peter looked at each other. It was time to let Mrs. Peggy know the things that had been happening to Jane.

Printed in the United States
By Bookmasters